Time For A Tale

Compiled by Julia Eccleshare

Illustrated by Rowan Barnes-Murphy

Hodder
Children's
Books

a division of Hodder Headline plc

First published in Great Britain in 1996
by Hodder Children's Books

A Catalogue record for this book is available
from the British Library

ISBN 0 340 65578 X

Typeset by Avon Dataset Ltd, Bidford-on-Avon, Warks

Printed and bound in Great Britain by
Clays Ltd, St Ives plc

Hodder Children's Books
a division of Hodder Headline plc
338 Euston Road
London NW1 3BH

CONTENTS

WONDERFUL WORMS

by

Berlie Doherty

The day before yesterday, Tilly Mint and
Mrs Hardcastle went down to the park to
find some magic. They didn't say they were
going to find some magic, but that's what
Tilly thought. She felt it in her bones. The

birds were singing brightly in the trees, and fetching and carrying things for their nests.

But all Mrs Hardcastle seemed to be interested in was worms.

'Just look at that worm, Tilly!' she said, when they walked past a bed of earth that had just been turned. 'Just look at that blobby old worm!' Tilly didn't like worms.

'Eugh!' she said. 'I'm not going near a worm.'

Mrs Hardcastle was surprised. 'I thought everyone liked worms, Tilly Mint,' she said. 'Worms are wonderful.'

'How they wibble, and they wobble,
And they wubble all around,
How they dibble, and they dabble,
And they double up and down.

How they're pink, and how they're
  pokey,
How they pull across the ground,
How they wind, and how they wander,
How they wiggle round and round!'

'Not to me, they're not,' said Tilly. 'That worm's got nowhere to go. He looks bored. He's like a piece of string without a parcel.'

'He's like a shoe-lace looking for a shoe,' laughed Mrs Hardcastle.

'He's like a piece of spaghetti that nobody wants to eat,' said Tilly Mint.

'Don't you be so sure about that!' Mrs Hardcastle said. 'Somebody wants to eat him. Look!'

Just above them, on the branch of a high tree, sat a little brown bird, singing his head off. His eyes were as bright as buttons. He

3

was watching the worm. Suddenly he flew down from the branch, and he hopped across to where the worm was wriggling about with nowhere to go, looking bored.

'Look out!' shouted Mrs Hardcastle to the worm. But she was too late. The hoppity bird had put his beak right round the worm. The worm tried to wiggle back down into the earth. The brown bird dug his feet in, and pulled and pulled and pulled. The pink worm stretched and stretched and stretched.

And suddenly, POP! Out came the worm. The brown bird fell over; then he stood up, shook his feathers, and flew off with the worm waving helplessly in his beak.

'Hooray!' Mrs Hardcastle clapped her hands.

Now it was Tilly who was surprised. 'I

thought you liked worms, Mrs Hardcastle,'
she said.

'So I do,' Mrs Hardcastle said. 'But I like
birds more. Just think of those little baby
birds, all snug and warm in their nest,
waiting for their tea. They'll be very
pleased when they see that worm.'

I wouldn't mind being a baby bird, all
snug and warm in a nest, thought Tilly. But
I'd jump right out of it if anyone gave me
worms for my tea. Fancy eating a worm!

'I nearly ate a worm once, Tilly Mint,
when I was a little girl. But oh, that was so
long ago. That was years and years and
years ago. I've nearly forgotten all about it.'

And when Mrs Hardcastle said that, it
was in her drowsy, far-away, remembery
sort of voice, and her eyes seemed to be
looking into long, long ago. Then she sat

down on a park bench, closed them, and she fell asleep and snored.

'Crumbs!' said Tilly. 'I'm in for it now! Magic-time!'

She closed her eyes, and when she opened them, she was in a dark, dark place. She seemed to be in a tiny, little, dark room, with hard, smooth, warm walls, and it was round.

'No, it isn't!' said Tilly, after a bit. 'It's not round! It's egg-shaped. I must be . . . inside . . . an egg!'

She pushed her head up against the top of her egg, and the shell began to crack. She pushed her arms out against the sides of her egg, and the shell began to crunch. She pushed her feet out through the bottom of her egg, and the shell began to crack, crunch, crumble!

And she was out into the air, into the sunshine, into the lovely blue light that was full of the song of birds.

Tilly took a deep breath and looked round her. Three fluffy birds were standing next to her, blinking in the sunlight. They were all standing on bits of shell. And underneath the bits of shell, there was straw, and grass, and twigs, and leaves, all plaited together like a warm, snug hat. They were in a nest!

Tilly hopped to the side of it and looked down. The nest seemed to be right at the top of the highest tree in the world. The branches began to sway in the wind.

'I'm hungry!' cheeped all the baby birds. 'Very hungry.'

So am I! thought Tilly. Very, very hungry.

Just then, the brown bird hopped on to the

side of the nest. Tilly recognised him by his eyes that were as bright as buttons, and by his dirty feet, and by the pink worm that was wriggling about in his beak. The baby birds pushed each other over in excitement.

Tilly remembered what Mrs Hardcastle had told her about the wonderful worms:

'How they wibble, and they wobble,
And they wubble all around,
How they dibble, and they dabble,
And they double up and down.
How they're pink, and how they're
*   pokey,*
How they prowl across the ground,
How they wind, and how they wander,
How they wiggle round and round!'

The brown bird saw that Tilly had her

mouth open, and he hopped over to her, and started to lower the worm into her beak!

'Oh no!' said Tilly. 'I'm not that hungry! I'm not having worms for my tea!'

She took the poor old worm very gently into her beak, and climbed up on to the side of the nest. She looked down from the top of the highest tree in the world.

'Bird in a nest on a branch in a tree,
Sail in the wind like a ship on the sea.
Worm in the beak of the bird in the
   skies,
Point to the ground, and close your
   eyes!'

Tilly Mint spread out her fluffy, feathery arms, and she closed her eyes that were as bright as buttons, and she jumped. She floated down, and down, and down.

And when she opened her eyes again, she was standing on the soft, brown earth with the little, pink worm in her hand. She knelt down and put him on the earth.

'In you go, little worm,' she whispered. 'You pop down there, and don't come out again till night-time.'

The worm tucked his head into the soil and slithered out of sight.

Suddenly, Tilly remembered Mrs Hardcastle, fast asleep and snoring in the sunshine. She shook her arms to make quite sure there were no feathers left on, and then she woke up Mrs Hardcastle.

'Wake up, Mrs Hardcastle!' she said. 'I'm ever so hungry.'

Mrs Hardcastle opened her eyes. She looked at the blue sky, that was full of birdsong. She looked up at the branches of the tallest tree in the world, and saw, at the very top, a little nest, swaying in the wind like a boat on the sea. She looked at the brown birds, busy with their fetching and carrying.

'Hello, Tilly Mint!' she said. And then she said: 'Let's go home, shall we, and have our tea.'

And they did.

by

Catherine Storr

Once every two weeks Polly went over to
the other side of the town to see her
grandmother. Sometimes she took a small
present, and sometimes she came back with
a small present for herself. Sometimes all

13

the rest of the family went too, and sometimes Polly went alone.

One day, when she was going by herself, she had hardly got down the front door steps when she saw the wolf.

'Good afternoon, Polly,' said the wolf. 'Where are you going to, may I ask?'

'Certainly,' said Polly. 'I'm going to see my grandma.'

'I thought so!' said the wolf, looking very much pleased. 'I've been reading about a little girl who went to visit her grandmother and it's a very good story.'

'Little Red Riding Hood?' suggested Polly.

'That's it!' cried the wolf. 'I read it out loud to myself as a bed-time story. I did enjoy it. The wolf eats up the grandmother, *and* Little Red Riding Hood. It's almost the only story where a wolf really gets anything to eat,' he added sadly.

'But in my book he doesn't get Red Riding Hood,' said Polly. 'Her father comes in just in time to save her.'

'Oh, he doesn't in *my* book!' said the wolf. 'I expect mine is the true story, and yours is just invented. Anyway, it seems a good idea.'

'What is a good idea?' asked Polly.

'To catch little girls on their way to their grandmothers' cottages,' said the wolf. 'Now where had I got to?'

'I don't know what you mean,' said Polly.

'Well, I'd said, "Where are you going to?"' said the wolf. 'Oh yes. Now I must say "Where does she live?" Where does your grandmother live, Polly Riding Hood?'

'Over the other side of town,' answered Polly.

The wolf frowned.

'It ought to be "Through the Wood",' he said. 'But perhaps town will do. How do you get there, Polly Riding Hood?'

'First I take a train and then I take a bus,' said Polly.

The wolf stamped his foot.

'No, no, no, no!' he shouted. 'That's all wrong. You can't say that. You've got to say, "By that path winding through the trees", or something like that. You can't go by trains and buses and things. It isn't fair.'

'Well, I could say that,' said Polly, 'but it wouldn't be true. I do have to go by bus and train to see my grandma, so what's the good of saying I don't?'

'But then it won't work,' said the wolf

impatiently. 'How can I get there first and gobble her up and get all dressed up to trick you into believing I am her, if we've got a great train journey to do? And anyhow I haven't any money on me, so I can't even take a ticket. You just can't say that.'

'All right, I won't say it,' said Polly agreeably. 'But it's true all the same. Now just excuse me, Wolf, I've got to get down to the station because I am going to visit my grandma even if you aren't.'

The wolf slunk along behind Polly, growling to himself. He stood just behind her at the booking-office and heard her ask for her ticket, but he could not go any further. Polly got into a train and was carried away, and the wolf went sadly home.

But just two weeks later the wolf was

waiting outside Polly's house again. This time he had plenty of change in his pocket. He even had a book tucked under his front leg to read in the train.

He partly hid himself behind a corner of a brick wall and watched to see Polly come out on her way to her grandmother's house.

But Polly did not come out alone, as she had before. This time the whole family appeared, Polly's father and mother too. They got into the car which was waiting in the road, and Polly's father started the engine.

The wolf ran along behind his brick wall as fast as he could, and was just in time to get out into the road ahead of the car, and to stand waving his paws as if he wanted a lift as the car came up.

Polly's father slowed down, and Polly's mother put her head out of the window.

'Where do you want to go?' she asked.

'I want to go to Polly's grandmother's house,' the wolf answered. His eyes glistened as he looked at the family of plump little girls in the back of the car.

'That's where we are going,' said her mother, surprised. 'Do you know her then?'

'Oh no,' said the wolf. 'But you see, I want to get there very quickly and eat her up and then I can put on her clothes and wait for Polly, and eat her up too.'

'Good heavens!' said Polly's father. 'What a horrible idea! We certainly shan't give you a lift if that is what you are planning to do.'

Polly's mother screwed up the window again and Polly's father drove quickly on.

The wolf was left standing miserably in the road.

'Bother!' he said to himself angrily. 'It's gone wrong again. I can't think why it can't be the same as the Little Red Riding Hood story. It's all these buses and cars and trains that make it go wrong.'

But the wolf was determined to get Polly, and when she was due to visit her grandmother again, a fortnight later, he went down and took a ticket for the station he had heard Polly ask for. When he got out of the train, he climbed on a bus, and soon he was walking down the road where Polly's grandmother lived.

'Aha!' he said to himself, 'this time I shall get them both. First the grandma, then Polly.'

He unlatched the gate into the garden,

and strolled up the path to Polly's grandmother's front door. He rapped sharply with
the knocker.

'Who's there?' called a voice from inside
the house.

The wolf was very much pleased. This
was going just as it had in the story. This
time there would be no mistakes.

'Little Polly Riding Hood,' he said in a
squeaky voice. 'Come to see her dear
grandmother, with a little present of butter
and eggs and – er – cake!'

There was a long pause. Then the voice
said doubtfully, '*Who* did you say it was?'

'Little Polly Riding Hood,' said the wolf
in a great hurry, quite forgetting to disguise
his voice this time. 'Come to eat up her dear
grandmother with butter and eggs!'

There was an even longer pause. Then

Polly's grandmother put her head out of the window and looked down at the wolf.

'I beg your pardon?' she said.

'I am Polly,' said the wolf firmly.

'Oh,' said Polly's grandma. She appeared to be thinking hard. 'Good afternoon, Polly. Do you know if anyone else happens to be coming to see me today? A wolf for instance?'

'No. Yes,' said the wolf in great confusion. 'I met a Polly as I was coming here – I mean, I, Polly, met a wolf on my way here, but she can't have got here yet because I started specially early.'

'That's very odd,' said the grandma. 'Are you quite sure you are Polly?'

'Quite sure,' said the wolf.

'Well, then, I don't know who it is who is here already,' said Polly's grandma. 'She said she was Polly. But if you are Polly then I think this other person must be a wolf.'

'No, no, I am Polly,' said the wolf. 'And, anyhow, you ought not to say all that. You ought to say "Lift the latch and come in".'

'I don't think I'll do that,' said Polly's grandma. 'Because I don't want my nice little Polly eaten up by a wolf, and if you come in now the wolf who is here already might eat you up.'

Another head looked out of the window. It was Polly's.

'Bad luck, Wolf,' she said. 'You didn't know that I was coming to lunch and tea today instead of just tea as I generally do – so I got here first. And as you are Polly, as you've just said, I must be the wolf, and you'd better run away quickly before I gobble you up, hadn't you?'

'Bother, bother, bother and *bother*!' said the wolf. 'It hasn't worked out right this time either. And I did just what it said in the book. Why can't I ever get you, Polly, when that other wolf managed to get his little girl?'

'Because this isn't a fairy story,' said Polly, 'and I'm not Little Red Riding Hood, I am Polly and I can always escape from you, Wolf, however much you try to catch me.'

'Clever Polly,' said Polly's grandma. And the wolf went growling away.

by

John Yeoman

It was a terribly hot day in the jungle, and
all the birds and beasts, exhausted from the
heat, had curled up to sleep. The silence
was broken only by an occasional snapping
of twigs and beating of soft-feathered wings

25

as a parrot nearly slipped off its perch in a tall tree.

The only creature who couldn't sleep was a small brown monkey, who was very very thirsty indeed. He wandered on all fours through the lush green undergrowth in the hope of finding a small puddle. Every now and then he stopped and raised himself on to his back legs, peering this way and that for a tell-tale sparkle of sunlight on water. But it was useless, for it had been a very very long, hot, dry summer.

At last his search led him to the edge of the dark green jungle, to the place where the desert begins. He stopped again, blinking into the strong sunlight. But he knew that there was no chance at all of finding cool water in the desert.

But what was that he could see? Out there,

standing all by itself, was a tall, fat pot – just the sort of pot which might be expected to have water in it. With a bound the monkey was beside it. If he climbed on to a dead branch among the stones he could just manage to peer into the dark inside of the pot. Was there water in it? He couldn't see any water, but then, it was very dark in there. Gingerly he lowered a thin arm into the pot. His long sensitive fingers could feel a coolness which might mean that there was water farther down. So he very carefully lowered his hand farther, and farther, and farther, until he was standing on tiptoe and his arm was stretched as far as it would go. And then the very tips of his long fingers felt cold water.

And now what was he to do, may I ask? Just think: the water was so near, and yet so hard to reach!

'I will put my shoulder to the pot,' said the small brown monkey, gently scratching his lower lip with a long finger, 'and I will rock it until it tumbles over – and then I will drink the water.' And he put his thin bony shoulder against the pot, and pushed with all his might. Then he pushed again and again and again until – the pot began to rock. It rocked very little at first but gradually it swayed more and more and it seemed that the very next push would send it toppling over.

'Stop!' called a small voice. The small brown monkey stopped in surprise, and the pot gently rocked itself to a standstill. There was no one to be seen.

'Who said that?' asked the small brown monkey.

'I did,' said a green lizard, sliding quickly

from beneath the pot and raising his head towards the monkey. 'I live under this pot and I was trying to have a nap when you came and started making the ground shake. And why are you wearing that fur on a hot day like this?'

The monkey did not answer the last question and looked very ashamed.

'I am sorry to disturb you,' he said, 'but I wanted to drink that cool water. I can't reach it and so I must spill it on the ground before I can drink it.'

'Really, you ought to have more sense,' said the lizard. 'Just look at the ground.' And he whisked round in a flash, so that one moment he was facing one way and the next he was facing the other. 'It's all hot stone and dry dust,' he went on. 'If you spill the water then the ground will drink it all up before you could get a single drop. Think of something else and have the goodness to make less noise about it when other people are sleeping.' And with that he darted under the pot once more.

The small brown monkey sat down on the stones of the desert and looked at the pot again, and felt thirstier than ever.

He had been sitting for a few minutes with the sun beating down on him, when suddenly he felt cold. He noticed that he was now sitting in shadow, and looking up he saw a great black shape hovering over him.

'Who's that?' asked the monkey.

'I am a monkey-eating eagle,' said the big shape, coming nearer, 'and who are you?'

Now the small brown monkey knew what was good for him, and fortunately he was clever enough to have an answer ready. 'By a strange coincidence,' he replied quickly, 'I am an eagle-eating monkey, and I should be pleased to meet you.'

The big bird hastily rose several feet higher into the blue sky.

'Have you by any chance,' called the small brown monkey after him, 'seen any water about in your travels?'

'From up here I can see everything,' came the reply, 'and the only water that I can see is the hippopotamus's pond.' With that the great bird rose higher still. 'Second on the left past the mango tree and first right after the paw-paw tree.'

And with that the great bird soared up and up until it disappeared in the sky.

It was a hot and thirsty little monkey who trudged back into the stuffy green heat of the jungle. He followed the directions given to him, and at last arrived at the hippopotamus's pond. But what a disappointment awaited him! Instead of cool, fresh water, as he had hoped, there was thick, steaming, muddy water.

'Ugh! I can't drink that!' said the sad creature, and he squatted down on his hind quarters and cried.

Now the hippopotamus had seen and heard all this from her position in the middle of the pool. But because she was almost completely under the water (all except her eyes and her nostrils) the monkey hadn't noticed her. At first she had kept quite still because she had been a little offended – I may as well admit it – by the monkey's unwillingness to drink her beautiful bathwater. However, she was a tender-hearted old thing and as soon as the monkey began to cry, she floated to the surface and, garlanded with smelly pond-weed, swam to the bank.

'There, there,' she said comfortingly. 'Did you want a drink, then?'

The monkey looked up quickly and gazed at the large smiling face which greeted him. In fact, he rather forgot his manners and *stared* at it, fascinated by the bristles on her chin. But he quickly remembered himself and said: 'Good afternoon. Yes, I would very much like a drink, because I'm so hot and thirsty.'

'Then just wait for me to climb out and I'll help you search through the jungle for water,' said the hippopotamus.

It was such a well-meant and kind offer that the monkey felt he had to accept it, although he knew that apart from the water

33

in the pot, which he couldn't reach, there wasn't a single drop in the whole jungle.

So he waited for the hippopotamus to come out of the pond and she did. And what do you think! The monkey noticed, with his eyes wide open with delight, that as she climbed out of the pond, the level of the water slowly went down.

'Oh, please get in again!' called the monkey excitedly.

'But I want to help you,' insisted the hippopotamus.

'And so you will!' cried the small brown monkey.

With a puzzled look on her huge face, but nevertheless pleased to be useful, the hippopotamus sank slowly back into the water. Sure enough, as she did so the water rose again in the pond.

'Hurrah!' shouted the monkey, bounding away. Then remembering his manners again, he bounded back and said quietly: 'Thank you very much for helping me. I am most grateful to you.' And he ran off to the edge of the jungle.

Back at the pot he quickly collected an armful of big stones – the biggest he could find. He carried them to the side of the pot, climbed up on to the branch, and began to drop the stones in, ever so gently, one by one.

'Splash!' went the first one, faintly, as it hit the bottom.

'Splash!' went the next, a little louder.

And he dropped in more and more until the big pot was three-quarters filled with stones and – what do you think? – the water had risen to the very brim. All the monkey had to do then was to purse his lips and drink the fresh, cool water from the top of the pot.

'And when the water gets too low again,' he said happily to himself, 'I can always drop some more stones in.'

It's a clever monkey who uses his eyes and his common sense.

by
Lance Salway

A long time ago, in a far country, there lived a boy called Claud who was so bad that people both far and near had heard of his naughtiness. His mother and father loved him dearly, and so did his brothers and sisters, but even they became angry at the tricks he played on them and the mischief that he caused by his bad behaviour.

Once, when his grandmother came to stay, Claud put a big, fat frog in her bed. Once, when the teacher wasn't looking, he changed the hands on the school clock so that the children were sent home two hours early. And once, when Claud was feeling especially bad, he cut his mother's washing line so that the clean clothes fell into the mud, and he poured a bottle of ink over the head of his eldest sister, and he locked his two young brothers into a cupboard and threw the key down a well. And, as if that wasn't bad enough, he climbed to the top of the tallest tree in the garden and tied his father's best shirt to the topmost branch so that it waved in the wind like a flag.

His parents and his brothers and sisters did all they could to stop Claud's mischief and to make him a better boy. They sent him to bed without any supper, but that didn't make any difference. They wouldn't let him go to the circus when it came to the town, but that didn't make any difference. They wouldn't let him go out to play with his friends, but that didn't make any difference either because Claud hadn't any friends. All the other boys and girls of the town were much too frightened to play with him and, in any case, their parents wouldn't let them. But Claud didn't mind. He liked to play tricks on people and he enjoyed being as bad as possible. And he laughed when his parents became cross or his brothers and sisters cried because he liked to see how angry they would get when he was naughty.

'What *are* we to do with you?' sighed his mother. 'We've tried everything we can think of to stop you being so naughty. And it hasn't made any difference at all.'

'But I enjoy being bad,' said Claud, and he pushed his youngest sister so hard that she fell on the floor with a thump.

Everybody in the town had heard of Claud's naughtiness, and it wasn't long before the news spread to the next town and the next until everyone had heard that Claud was the naughtiest boy in the land. The king and queen had heard of Claud's naughtiness. And even the Chief Witch, who was the oldest and the ugliest and the most wicked witch in the kingdom, had heard of him too.

One day, the Chief Witch came to visit Claud's parents. They were very frightened when they saw her but Claud was over-joyed, especially when she told him that if he promised to be very bad indeed she would allow him to ride on her broomstick.

'I believe your son is the naughtiest boy in the whole country,' she said to Claud's father.

'He is,' he replied, sadly.

'Good!' said the Witch. 'I would like him to join my school for bad children. We are always looking for clever children to train as witches and wizards. And the naughtier they are, the better.'

Claud was very pleased when he heard of the Witch's plan and he begged his parents to allow him to go to her school.

'At least we'd have some peace,' said his mother. 'Yes, you may as well go, if it will make you happy.'

'Oh, it will, it will!' shouted Claud, and he rushed upstairs to get ready for the journey. And so, a few days later, the Chief Witch called again on her broomstick to take Claud to her school. He said goodbye to his parents and his brothers and sisters and climbed on to the broomstick behind her. He couldn't wave to his family but he smiled happily at them as he flew away on the long journey to school, clutching the broomstick with one hand and holding his suitcase with the other.

Everybody was pleased to see him go. The people of the town were pleased. Claud's brothers and sisters were pleased.

'Now we can enjoy ourselves,' they said. 'Claud won't be here to play tricks on us now.'

Even his mother and father were pleased.

'He'll be happy with the Witch,' they said. 'He can be as bad as he likes now.'

But, as time passed, they found that they all missed Claud.

'It was much more fun when he was here,' complained his brothers and sisters. 'We never knew what would happen next.'

Claud's mother and father, too, began to wish that he had never gone away. Even though he was such a bad boy they loved him dearly and wished that they had never allowed the Chief Witch to take him to school. And the people of the town wished that Claud would come back.

'There was never a dull moment when Claud was here,' they sighed. 'Now, nothing ever happens in our town.'

As the weeks passed, Claud's family missed him more and more.

'Perhaps he'll come back to visit us,' his mother said.

But the summer ended and the autumn passed and then winter came but still there was no visit from Claud.

'He'll never come back,' said his father, sadly.

And then, on a cold night in the middle of winter, they heard a faint knock on the front door.

'I wonder who that can be,' said Claud's mother, as she went to open it. 'Why, it's Claud!' she cried. And it was. He stood shivering on the doorstep, looking very thin and miserable and cold.

'We're so glad you've come back,' said his father. 'Sit down and tell us what happened and why you've come back to us.'

'I wasn't bad enough,' Claud said, and burst into tears. And then, when he had been given something to eat and had warmed himself by the fire, he told his parents about the school and about the very wicked children who were there.

'They were even naughtier than I am,' he said. 'They turned people into frogs. They turned *me* into a frog until the Witch told them to turn me back. They were much, much naughtier than me. And even though I tried very hard indeed I just couldn't be as bad as the others. And so the Witch said I was too good ever to become a wicked wizard and she sent me away.'

'Never mind,' said his parents. 'We're very pleased to see you. We've missed you.'

His brothers and sisters were overjoyed at

Claud's return. They laughed when Claud filled their shoes with jam while they were asleep. And they laughed when Claud tied them all to a tree. They even laughed when he pushed them all into the goldfish pond.

'Good old Claud!' they shouted. 'We're glad you're back!'

His mother laughed when she found out he had put beetles into the tea caddy. And his father didn't seem to mind when Claud cut large holes in his newspaper.

'Claud's back and quite his old self again,' they said, and smiled at each other.

But soon Claud found that being naughty wasn't as much fun any more. 'Nobody seems to mind my tricks,' he complained, 'even the new ones I learned at the Witch's school. People laugh when I trip them up, or tie their shoelaces together, or put ants in their hair. Why can't they be as angry as they used to be?'

So, because being bad wasn't any fun any more, Claud decided to be good instead. Not *completely* good, of course. Every now and again he would throw mud at his brothers and once he even covered the cat with a mixture of shoe polish and marmalade. But people soon forgot that he was once the naughtiest boy in the whole country. And the Chief Witch was so disappointed in Claud that she didn't call again.

by

Linda Allen

'Stanley,' said Mrs Simkin to Mr Simkin one day, 'there's a pig under the bed.'

'What colour is it?' asked Mr Simkin.

Mrs Simkin looked again.

'It's a pink one,' she said.

'Then we must find out who it belongs to,' said Mr Simkin. 'We can't have a pink pig under the bed.'

Mr Simkin went to ask his friend if he had lost a pink pig.

'No,' said his friend. 'I lost half a pound of dripping once, on a bus, but I have never lost a pink pig.'

'Then it can't be yours,' said Mr Simkin.

Mrs Simkin mentioned it in passing to the lady next door. The lady next door said she was expecting a Shetland pony next week.

Mr Robinson, who lived across the street, said he had a water buffalo in his green-house.

'Stanley,' said Mrs Simkin, 'I really think we shall have to keep the little pink pig. If it doesn't belong to your friend, and the lady next door doesn't want it, and Mr Robinson prefers his water buffalo, what else can we do?'

'But whatever can we call it?' asked Mr Simkin.

'Marcia,' said Mrs Simkin. 'That's a nice name for a pig.'

So they brought a little blue bonnet for Marcia and a ladder in case she wanted to climb the apple tree.

Mr Simkin built her a garage to sit in. Marcia was very happy.

On Mr Simkin's birthday Mrs Simkin said to him, 'Stanley, there's another pig under the bed.'

'Is it another pink one?' asked Mr Simkin.

'Yes,' said Mrs Simkin.

'Then she can sit in the garage with Marcia,' said Mr Simkin.

So they named the new little pig

Veronica, after the lady next door, and Veronica sat in the garage with Marcia, and they had conversations.

Mr Simkin went to see his friend again. 'Have you lost a pink pig yet?' he asked.

'No,' he said. 'I haven't found my half pound of dripping yet either.'

'Never mind,' said Mr Simkin. 'I'm sure you will one day.'

Mr Robinson built an extension to his greenhouse. 'I wonder if Mr Robinson has found another water buffalo in his greenhouse?'

Mr Robinson didn't talk to Mr and Mrs Simkin very much.

Mrs Simkin found another pink pig under the bed on Shrove Tuesday. She found another one on the day that her niece won a prize for leaping over a wheelbarrow. Mrs

52

Simkin found a lot of pigs.

'You'll have to clean under the bed more regularly,' said Mr Simkin to Mrs Simkin.

'I do,' said Mrs Simkin, 'but every time I clean under the bed I find another pig there.'

Soon they had forty-seven pigs.

Mr Robinson didn't talk to them at all now.

The lady next door rode away on her Shetland pony.

The garage was quite full of little pink pigs. There were no more blue bonnets anywhere in town, and Mr Simkin had to climb over all the ladders when he wanted to go out.

'It's not that I don't *like* pink pigs,' he told his wife one day, 'but it *is* rather inconvenient having so many. Shall we give some of them away?'

'Oh, no, Stanley,' said Mrs Simkin. 'That would never do.'

'Then there's only one thing to be done,' said Mr Simkin. 'We'll have to sell the bed.'

'Sell the bed!' exclaimed Mrs Simkin.

'It's the only way,' her husband said.

Mrs Simkin was sad.

'Do you want to buy a bed?' Mr Simkin asked a man in the park.

'Oh, yes!' he said. 'Why do you want to sell it?'

'We keep finding pink pigs underneath it,' said Mr Simkin.

'I don't mind that,' said the man.

He went to the house with Mr Simkin and looked at the bed. 'It's a very nice bed,' he said, and he took the bed away.

Mrs Simkin bought a new bed. It was a lovely bed. It had large brass knobs on it. There were no pink pigs underneath it.

Mr Simkin and Mrs Simkin and the forty-seven pink pigs were very happy all living all together.

Mrs Simkin used to clean underneath the new bed every day.

'Stanley,' said Mrs Simkin one morning, 'isn't it strange? There's a pig under the new bed.'

'What!' cried Mr Simkin. 'Our new bed! Another pink pig?'

'Oh, no, dear,' said Mrs Simkin as she shook her duster, 'this one is a black one.'

Mr Simkin sighed with relief. 'That's all right then,' he said.

THE BIGGEST-CREAM-BUN IN THE WORLD

by

Mary Danby Calvert

Big Fat Rosie was the biggest, fattest person there ever was.

She was bigger than a barrel. She was plumper than a pudding. She was rounder than a rubber ball. And almost as heavy as a

57

medium-sized hippopotamus.

And Big Fat Rosie was very, very wide. She was so wide that: She had to sit on an extra-wide chair. She had to sleep in an extra-wide bed. She had to eat with an extra-wide spoon.

And all the doors in her house were extra-wide, so that she could move from room to room without getting stuck.

Everything that Big Fat Rosie did was done enormously. When she ate (with her extra-wide spoon), she made a noise like this ompa chompa ompa chompa.

When she slept (in her extra-wide bed), she snored like this cor-fyoooo cor-fyooooo and all the walls quivered.

When she cried, like this OWO-WO-WO OWO-WO-WO such huge tears fell from her eyes that everything around her became soaking wet.

Big Fat Rosie was a farmer's wife, and her husband was called Turnip Tom. While Rosie looked after the house, Turnip Tom managed everything around the farm. He had pigs and cows and ducks and chickens and he grew wheat, cabbages, potatoes and, of course, turnips. Turnip Tom was very good to Big Fat Rosie and bought her plenty of nice things to eat. This made Big Fat Rosie happy, because she was very greedy indeed – and her favourite food was cream buns.

One day, when Turnip Tom was out working in the fields, Big Fat Rosie thought she would give him a surprise. She would make a great big cream bun and they could eat it together for their tea. She giggled happily, like this Ki Ki Ki Ki and made a list of all the things she would need: flour, eggs, milk, butter, sugar and cream.

There were big bags of flour and sugar in the larder, but the other ingredients would have to be collected from the farm.

Big Fat Rosie put on her rubber farm boots and went first to the cowshed, where Old Harry, the farm-boy, was putting hay in the cow's manger. Outside, the cows made hungry, waiting noises, like this mooooo mooooooo mooooo.

'Hallo, Harry,' said Big Fat Rosie. 'Please may I have some milk and some butter and some cream? I'm going to make the biggest cream bun in the world.'

'Arr,' said Harry, scratching his head. 'When a bun's big as that, there'll be some as gets fat.'

'Yes,' agreed Rosie, laughing cosily, 'me.' (Because, of course, she was already as fat as a couple of eiderdowns.)

Harry went into the dairy and came out with a can of milk, a bowl of butter and a jug of cream. Big Fat Rosie thanked him and trotted off towards the henhouse to look for some eggs.

When the hens saw her, they made a fearful racket, like this cookerookeroo cookerookeroo roo and flapped about her feet.

'No, no!' cried Big Fat Rosie. 'It isn't tea-time yet. I've come to fetch some eggs.' She went over to the nesting boxes and looked inside. There were ten beautiful speckly-brown eggs, some of them still warm. She put them in her apron pocket and walked carefully back to the farmhouse, trying not to bump them with her knees. Hee hee! she thought. Now I can make the biggest cream bun in the world.

When the mixture was ready in the bowl, Big Fat Rosie stirred it with her wooden spoon, like this slurrp slurrp and licked her lips. She tasted the mixture twenty-six times, just to be sure it was right, and added a few spoonfuls of yeast. Yeast would make the bun rise splendidly, like a loaf of bread. Turnip Tom *would* be pleased.

Big Fat Rosie bent down to light the oven. It made a noise like this POP POP and she poured the bun mixture on to the biggest baking tray she could find. When she had placed it in the oven, she sat in her very wide rocking chair and hummed a little happy tune as she rocked, like this dum

dum di dum dumetty dumetty
dum.

And then she fell asleep.

In the oven, the bun was rising higher and
higher. In the chair, Rosie was snoring
louder and louder, like this cor-fyoo
cor-fyoo.

The whole kitchen was shaking with the
noise – until suddenly the oven door burst
open with a bang. Big Fat Rosie woke up,
rubbed her eyes and looked around her.
What on earth was that peculiar sound? It
went like this Splobble Splobble.

It was the bun! It was pouring out of the
oven! Over the floor it crept steadily,
blobbing and bubbling, slopping and
slurping.

It looked as though it would never stop.
But Big Fat Rosie was not going to be

beaten by a bun. She knew she could never sweep it up – but she could eat it. It was almost time for tea, anyway. She grabbed the nearest piece and began to eat very fast, like this ompa chompa ompa chompa.

But the bun kept on coming. It was rising up the table legs and Big fat Rosie had to eat even faster, like this ompa chompa ompa chompa. She wished she had never put all that yeast in the mixture.

Then the bun began to creep over the window sill and out into the garden. Turnip Tom, coming home from the fields, called out to Harry.

'Come quick! There's a bun climbing out of the window!'

'Dearie me,' said Harry and hurried with him to the kitchen. There they found Big

Fat Rosie knee deep in bun, eating more and more slowly, like this om-pah-chom-pah.

'Omp,' she mumbled, almost in tears. 'It was going – omp – to be the biggest chomp bomp in the womp.'

'Never mind,' said Turnip Tom, who always knew exactly what to do, 'Harry and I can take it away in a barrow.'

'Arr,' said Harry.

They fetched their shovels and a wheelbarrow and began to scrape the cream bun off the walls. Harry switched off the oven and the rest of the dough began to sink.

Finally, it stopped. Turnip Tom gave a great big sigh of relief, like this whee-yew and stood looking thoughtfully at the barrowload of bun. 'We could bury it in the garden,' he suggested.

Harry said: 'When a bun gets too big, remember the pig.'

So they gave the bun to Alexander, who was always hungry, and he grunted happily, like this oinker oinker oink as if to say, 'Thank you very much.'

But Big fat Rosie thought he was saying, 'What a rotten cook' and decided she would make another biggest cream bun in the world tomorrow, just to show him. And this time it would be even bigger.

by

Joan Aiken

Once, long ago when you could get four
ounces of fruit drops for a penny, and might
easily see half a dozen horses between you
and the house on the other side of the street,
there was a tree that loved a girl.

67

This happened in a village so small that there were only nine houses in it. They were grouped in a ring, and the tree, which was a huge oak, stood in the middle, and spread its branches over all of them like an umbrella.

The girl, whose name was Polly, lived in one of the houses. While she was a baby, her mother used to leave her out in her cradle under the oak tree, and there she would lie, kicking her feet and waving her fists and looking up at the sunshine coming through hundreds of the green leaves above her. And the oak tree looked down and thought that Polly was the prettiest baby in the world. She had blue eyes, brown hair, and pink cheeks.

When Polly grew a little older, she used to bring her skipping rope, or roller-skates, and skip or skate under the tree. And she played dolls' tea parties with the acorn cups, or hide and seek with her friends, round the oak tree's enormous trunk. Even if it was a pouring-wet day, the oak tree took care that no drop of rain should fall on Polly.

And then, when Polly was a little older, she used to bring her lesson books after school and sit doing her homework under the tree while it shaded her with its branches from the hot sun.

And later, when the girls of the village washed their clothes in the fountain, Polly would be there too, and the oak tree looked at her and loved her the best. When she had washed all her hair ribbons – red, blue, green, yellow and pink – she would hang them on a branch to dry. And the oak tree took care that they should not be blown away, or stolen by nest-building birds.

In autumn, the branches over Polly's house were always the last to lose their leaves, and in spring they were the first to bud.

But girls grow faster than trees. After what seemed only a few months to the oak tree, Polly grew up, and she went away to the city to seek her fortune.

At first the oak tree could not believe that she had left. But there were no ribbons hanging on the branches to dry at night, no books laid out on the grass among its roots, no Polly playing hide and seek with her friends round the huge, wrinkled trunk when homework was finished. She was truly gone.

The tree began to mourn. Although it was

no later than midsummer, leaves began falling from its branches. Birds who had built their nests among the twigs became anxious.

'How can we protect our fledgelings from hawks and owls, once the leaves have fallen?' they asked.

A wood dove flew to the top of the tree, and asked it, 'Dear Tree, what is the matter? Why do you drop your leaves in the middle of summer? Is some worm gnawing at your roots? Can we do anything to help you?'

'I am sad because Polly has gone away. I haven't the heart to send out sap to keep my leaves green, now that she is no longer here to see them. No, there is nothing you can do for me.'

And the oak tree sighed deeply, as if a great gust of wind had blown through its branches. A thousand leaves fluttered off and scattered like flakes of snow. All the branches moved, and stretched yearningly in the direction of the city where Polly had gone.

'Why don't you send her a message asking her to come back?' asked the practical wood dove.

'I will send her a thousand messages,' said the oak tree.

All the leaves that had fallen drifted on the breeze to the city where Polly now lived. Wherever she walked oak leaves drifted down and touched her softly, as if begging her to return home. But Polly did not understand the oak tree's message.

'It is very strange,' she said, 'that all these oak leaves keep falling on me when there is no tree anywhere near.'

'You must try something else,' said the wood dove to the tree, when Polly did not come.

So the tree sent a dream to the village carpenter – whose house stood nearest to its trunk – asking him to cut off a branch, and make it into a gift for Polly. Losing a branch was dreadful to the tree. As the saw bit deeper, the oak tree trembled and groaned. But at last the branch was off, and the carpenter turned it into a beautiful rocking chair.

'Go to the city and find Polly,' the oak tree had begged him in his dream, 'give her the chair with my love, and beseech her to come home.' So the carpenter put the chair on a mule, and rode to the city. But when he arrived there, he thought, 'I could sell this handsome chair for enough to buy a new mule. Why should I run errands for the tree? Why should I trouble to search for the girl?'

So that is what he did. The wood dove had flown after him, saw what happened, and told the oak tree. The tree was so angry that another of its branches cracked down, split with rage, and fell on the carpenter's roof. When he returned home with his new mule, he found his house in ruins.

And the oak tree's leaves continued to fall.

'What shall we do now?' said the birds.

They asked the advice of the mistletoe, which hung in the oak tree's topmost fork. The mistletoe was growing anxious, for if the tree died, it, too, would be homeless.

'Pick enough of my berries to make a necklace,' it said. 'And carry that to Polly.'

So the birds picked a hundred beautiful

pearly mistletoe berries, and strung a necklace on a stem of grass, and the wood dove carried it to the city, looked for Polly, who was walking in the street, then skilfully dropped the necklace over her head.

'My goodness! Who has sent me this beautiful present?' said Polly.

But she never guessed that it was the oak tree who had sent it.

Meantime the tree waited, growing sadder and sadder.

'At least keep your leaves on till our fledgelings have flown,' begged the birds.

So the tree agreed to do this. But all the leaves turned brown, as if winter had come; only the mistletoe remained green in the topmost fork.

Now a young man saw Polly walking along the city street, wearing her beautiful pearl-coloured necklace, and he, like the oak tree, thought she was the prettiest girl in the world. So he asked her to marry him and she said yes. They had their wedding in the city, and the wood dove watched from the church steeple, and was dreadfully troubled, for now it seemed unlikely that Polly would ever return home.

But the wood dove was wrong.

For when Polly's new husband said to her, 'How many children shall we have? And where shall we live?' Polly remembered the oak tree beneath which she had lain in her cradle, which had kept her dry from the rain while she played with her friends, and sheltered her from the sun while she did her schoolwork; suddenly she became homesick for the place where she had been born.

'Let us go back to my village,' she said to her husband.

So they bought a mule, and on the first day of autumn, when the leaves, red, golden, and brown, were beginning to blow from the trees, they came riding back. The carpenter had left his ruined home and gone away, so Polly and her husband repaired the house and moved into it.

At first the oak tree could hardly believe its good fortune.

But when it understood that Polly had truly come back to live in the village, the sap started running through its veins, and dripped down like tears of joy. New pink buds and new green leaves began to sprout from its twigs, just when the other trees were losing their leaves, and, all winter long, the oak tree remained green from happiness.

Next summer Polly had a baby of her own. She put it out under the oak tree in its cradle, and the oak tree looked down at the baby's brown hair, blue eyes, and pink cheeks, and thought, 'That is the prettiest baby in the world.'

by

Hilda Carson

Once there was a little lion who lived in the forest with his father and mother.

When Father Lion had been out hunting, and roared to let Mother Lion know he was coming home, you could hear him all over the forest. And when Mother Lion roared back, you could hear *her* all over the forest. But the little lion had just a little voice.

'Never mind,' said Mother Lion. 'As you grow bigger, your voice will grow bigger, too.'

But it didn't.

One day Uncle Lion came to visit.

'We are glad to see you,' roared Mother Lion.

'Where have you been all this time?' roared Father Lion.

'Been on my summer holiday hunting trip,' roared Uncle Lion. 'And how are you, young fellow?'

'Very well, thank you,' said the little lion in his little voice.

'Bless my soul!' said Uncle Lion. 'What's the matter? Lost your voice?'

'Not all of my voice,' said the little lion. 'Just my roar.'

'High time you found it!' said Uncle Lion.

The little lion sat down and thought about what Uncle Lion had said, and after a while, when the grown-ups were busy talking, he went off into the forest, all by himself.

He saw some monkeys playing in the branches of a tall tree.

'Excuse me, please,' said the little lion politely, 'I've lost my voice. Not all of my voice, just my roar. Do you know where I might find it?'

The monkeys laughed till they almost fell out of the tree.

'Look at the lion without a roar!' they shouted. 'Listen to his little voice! Say something more, lion!' And they swung upside down from the branches, and threw twigs and leaves down on him.

'I think you're very rude,' said the little lion in his little voice, and he went away, out of the trees and down to the river.

At the edge of the river he found Mr Hippopotamus dozing in a nice warm squishy mud bath.

'Excuse me, please,' said the little lion politely. 'I've lost my voice. Not all of my voice, just my roar.'

Mr Hippopotamus opened one eye. 'And a good thing, too,' he said. 'There's too much noise around here.'

'Do you know where I might find it?' asked the little lion.

'Certainly not,' said Mr Hippopotamus, 'and if I did, I wouldn't tell you.' And he went to sleep again.

The little lion went on through the forest till he found a pretty green snake curled up on top of a rock.

'Excuse me, please,' he said politely, 'I've lost my voice. Not all of my voice, just my roar. Do you know where I might find it?'

The little snake uncurled herself slowly.

'Yes-s-s,' she said at last. 'I think I know the very place where you might find your roar, but it's in a very dangerous-s-s part of the forest.'

'I don't mind,' said the little lion, bravely.

'Follow me, then,' said the snake. 'This-s-s way.'

And she slipped down from the rock and slid away among the trees so fast that the little lion had to run to keep up with her.

Soon they came to a part of the forest where the little lion had never been before. The trees were very tall and very close together, so that it was dark underneath them, and the bushes were so thick that there was no path through them.

'This-s-s is the place,' said the little snake, and she slid into the bushes and disappeared.

'Come back!' said the little lion. 'Don't leave me alone here!'

But the little green snake didn't come back.

'Mother!' said the little lion in his little voice. 'Mother! I don't know where I am! I think I'm lost!'

But of course Mother Lion couldn't hear him.

The little lion sat down and looked round

him. It was very dark and very lonely, and he was very frightened.

So he cried. And he howled. And he ROARED.

And from far away in the forest Mother Lion roared back, 'I'm here, my little son! I'm coming!'

The little green snake slid out from under the bushes where she had been hiding all the time.

'I'm s-s-sorry I s-s-scared you,' she said, 'but I thought you'd find your roar if you ever *really* needed it.' And she disappeared again.

Then the three big lions came bounding through the forest to where the little lion was. Father Lion hugged him, and Mother Lion kissed him, and Uncle Lion said, 'Bless my soul, with a roar like that you should grow up to be the biggest lion in the forest.'

And they all went home together.

by

Aingelda Ardizzone

There was once a tiny doll who belonged to a girl who did not care for dolls.

For a long time she lay forgotten in a mackintosh pocket until one rainy day when the girl was out shopping.

The girl was following her mother round a grocer's shop when she put her hand in her pocket and felt something hard.

She took it out and saw it was the doll. 'Ugly old thing,' she said and quickly put it back again, as she thought, into her pocket.

But, in fact, since she didn't want the doll, she dropped it unnoticed into the deep freeze among the frozen peas.

The tiny doll lay quite still for a long time, wondering what was to become of her. She felt so sad, partly because she did not like being called ugly and partly because she was lost.

It was very cold in the deep freeze and the tiny doll began to feel rather stiff, so she decided to walk about and have a good look at the place. The floor was crisp and white, just like frost on a winter's morning. There were many packets of peas piled one on top of the other. They seemed to her like great big buildings. The cracks between the piles were rather like narrow streets.

She walked one way and then the other, passing, not only packets of peas, but packets of sliced beans, spinach, broccoli and mixed vegetables. Then she turned a corner and found herself among beef rissoles and fish fingers. However, she did not stop but went on exploring until she came to boxes of strawberries; and then ice-cream.

The strawberries reminded her of the time when she was lost once before among the strawberry plants in a garden. Then she sat all day in the sun smelling and eating strawberries.

Now she made herself as comfortable as

possible among the boxes.

The only trouble was that people were continually taking boxes out to buy them and the shop people were always putting in new ones.

At times it was very frightening. Once she was nearly squashed by a box of fish fingers.

The tiny doll had no idea how long she spent in the deep freeze. Sometimes it seemed very quiet. This, she supposed, was when the shop was closed for the night.

She could not keep count of the days.

One day when she was busy eating ice-cream out of a packet, she suddenly looked up and saw a little girl she had never seen before. The little girl was sorry for the tiny doll and wished she could take her home.

The doll looked so cold and lonely, but

the girl did not dare to pick her up because she had been told not to touch things in the shop. However, she felt she must do something to help the doll and as soon as she got home she set to work to make her some warm clothes.

First of all, she made her a warm bonnet out of a piece of red flannel.

This was a nice and easy thing to start with.

After tea that day she asked her mother to help her cut out a coat from a piece of blue velvet.

She stitched away so hard that she had just time to finish it before she went to bed. It was very beautiful.

The next day her mother said they were going shopping, so the little girl put the coat and bonnet in an empty matchbox and tied it into a neat parcel with brown paper and string.

She held the parcel tightly in her hand as she walked along the street.

As soon as she reached the shop she ran straight to the deep freeze to look for the tiny doll.

At first she could not see her anywhere. Then, suddenly, she saw her, right at the back, playing with the peas. The tiny doll was throwing them into the air and hitting them with an ice cream spoon.

The little girl threw in the parcel and the doll at once started to untie it. She looked very pleased when she saw what was inside.

She tried on the coat, and it fitted. She tried on the bonnet and it fitted too.

She jumped up and down with excitement

and waved to the little girl to say thank you.

She felt so much better in warm clothes and it made her feel happy to think that somebody cared for her.

Then she had an idea. She made the match box into a bed and pretended that the brown paper was a great big blanket. With a string she wove a mat to go beside the bed.

At last she settled down in the match box, wrapped herself in the brown paper blanket and went to sleep.

She had a long, long sleep because she was very tired and, when she woke up, she found that the little girl had been back again and had left another parcel. This time it contained a yellow scarf.

Now the little girl came back to the shop every day and each time she brought something new for the tiny doll. She made her a sweater, a petticoat, knickers with tiny frills, and gave her a little bit of a looking-glass to see herself in.

She also gave her some red tights which belonged to one of her own dolls to see if they would fit. They fitted perfectly.

At last the tiny doll was beautifully dressed and looked quite cheerful, but still nobody except the little girl ever noticed her.

'Couldn't we ask someone about the doll?' the little girl asked her mother. 'I would love to take her home to play with.'

The mother said she would ask the lady at the cash desk when they went to pay for their shopping.

'Do you know about the doll in the deep freeze?'

'No indeed,' the lady replied. 'There are no dolls in this shop.'

'Oh yes there are,' said the little girl and her mother, both at once. So the lady from the cash desk, the little girl and her mother all marched off to have a look. And there, sure enough, was the tiny doll down among the frozen peas.

'It's not much of a life for a doll in there,' said the shop lady, picking up the doll and giving it to the little girl. 'You had better take her home where she will be out of mischief.'

Having said this, she marched back to her desk with rather a haughty expression.

The little girl took the tiny doll home, where she lived for many happy years in a beautiful doll's house. The little girl played with her a great deal, but best of all the tiny doll liked the company of the other dolls. They all loved to listen to her adventures in the deep freeze.

by

Margaret Mayo

When the world was new and there was
magic everywhere – in lakes and mountains,
in rivers and rocks – in those times, the little
bluebird wasn't blue. He was grey. And the
coyote wasn't grey. He was green.

The little grey bird lived beside a lake, up in the mountains. It was a beautiful lake, always the same. Sunshine or rain, its water shone the bluest blue.

Every day the little grey bird flew round the lake, and he wished he was not such a dull grey colour, and he sang, over and over, 'Blue, blue, I wish I was blue!'

The Spirit of the Lake heard his song, and one night when the bird was asleep, the Spirit of the Lake came and whispered in his ear: 'If you want to be blue, jump in the lake, dip your head in the water and sing, "*Make me blue! Bluest blue water, make me blue!*" Every morning for four mornings you must do this, and then, little grey bird, you will see . . .'

When the little grey bird woke, he thought, 'What a lovely dream!' And he flew down to the lake, jumped in the water, dipped his head and sang, '*Make me blue! Bluest blue water, make me blue!*'

Then he flew up. But he was still grey. The next morning and the next, he did the same thing. But he was still grey.

On the fourth morning, just as he jumped in the water, the coyote strolled by, hungry as usual and looking for something to eat. The coyote watched the little grey bird jump in the water and dip his head. The coyote watched him fly up . . . *and what was this?* . . . suddenly the bird was BLUE!

The coyote called out, 'Hey! Bluebird! That was some magic! Tell me – how did you get to be blue?'

'Every morning for four days,' said the first bluebird that ever was, 'I jumped in the water, dipped my head and sang, "*Make me*

blue! Bluest blue water, make me blue!"
Then I flew up. And here I am, every feather
the bluest blue!'

Then the bluebird flew off singing a
happy song.

'That blue is the best colour ever,' said
the coyote. 'I think I'll change from green
to blue.'

So he jumped in the lake, dipped his head
and sang the song. He climbed up the bank,
had a good shake and lay in the sun to dry.
The next morning and the next, he did the
same thing.

On the fourth morning the coyote jumped
in the lake again, dipped his head and sang
the song. He climbed up the bank . . . and
he was BLUE! Every single hair was
BLUE!

'What a colour!' he gasped. 'I must go

and show everyone. The wolf and the dog . . . they will be so jealous. The raccoon . . . the possum . . . the bear . . . they will all wish they were blue like me!'

The coyote was in such a hurry to show everyone his new colour that he didn't wait to shake his coat dry. He just scooted off down the mountainside.

As he ran, he looked back at his blue tail and admired it. So he didn't notice the old tree stump, straight ahead, and he whammed into it, rolled over, and kept on rolling.

When he reached the bottom of the mountain, he was covered in dust. He scrambled to his feet and shook himself. He was still dusty. He shook himself some more. But the dust stayed.

After that, the coyote did a lot more

shaking. But, no matter how many times he shook himself, or how many times he jumped in the lake, dipped his head and sang, *the dust stayed*.

Even today, the coyote has a scruffy coat. It is dusty grey all over. But the bluebird is still the bluest blue. He kept his magic colour.

Acknowledgements

Every effort has been made by the publishers to trace the owners of the copyright in the stories in this book. If any are inadvertently wrongly attributed, we shall be happy to correct this in the event of a reprint. We gratefully acknowledge permission to reproduce copyright material by the following authors:

Wonderful Worms © Berlie Doherty from *Tilly Mint's Tales*, published by Methuen, reprinted by permission of Reed Consumer Books Ltd.
Little Polly Riding Hood © Catherine Storr from *Clever Polly and the Stupid Wolf*, published by Faber & Faber Ltd.
A Drink of Water © John Yeoman from *Stories for Five Year Olds*, published by Faber, 1973, reprinted by permission of A P Watt Ltd on behalf of John Yeoman.
The Boy Who Wasn't Bad Enough copyright © 1972 Lance Salway. Reproduced by permission

HODDER STORY COLLECTIONS

0 340 64632 2	BEST STORIES FOR UNDER FIVES	£2.99	❑
0 340 64633 0	BEST STORIES FOR FIVE YEAR OLDS	£2.99	❑
0 340 64634 9	BEST STORIES FOR SIX YEAR OLDS	£2.99	❑
0 340 64635 7	BEST STORIES FOR SEVEN YEAR OLDS	£2.99	❑
0 340 62657 7	FIVE MINUTES TO BED	£3.50	❑
0 340 65615 8	SIMPLY THE BEST	£3.99	❑
0 340 65146 6	COUNTRY TALES	£3.99	❑

BOOK AND TAPE PACKS

185998 3146	BEST STORIES FOR UNDER FIVES	£5.99	❑
185998 3154	BEST STORIES FOR FIVE YEAR OLDS	£5.99	❑
185998 3162	BEST STORIES FOR SIX YEAR OLDS	£5.99	❑
185998 3170	BEST STORIES FOR SEVEN YEAR OLDS	£5.99	❑
185998 4126	FIVE MINUTES TO BED	£5.99	❑

All Hodder Children's books are available at your local bookshop or newsagent, or can be ordered direct from the publisher. Just tick the titles you want and fill in the form below. Prices and availability subject to change without notice.

Hodder Children's Books, Cash Sales Department, Bookpoint, 39 Milton Park, Abingdon, OXON, OX14 4TD, UK. If you have a credit card you may order by telephone – (01235) 400414.

Please enclose a cheque or postal order made payable to Bookpoint Ltd to the value of the cover price and allow the following for postage and packing:
UK & BFPO – £1.00 for the first book, 50p for the second book, and 30p for each additional book ordered up to a maximum charge of £3.00.
OVERSEAS & EIRE – £2.00 for the first book, £1.00 for the second book, and 50p for each additional book.

Name ....

Address ....

....

....

If you would prefer to pay by credit card, please complete:
Please debit my Visa/Access/Diner's Card/American Express (delete as applicable) card no:

Signature ....

Expiry Date ....